OMG, what is this?
Why am I bleeding from my vagina?
I0726580

I can't get it to stop.
What? A period.
I do not want this, PERIODT!

# i DON'T WANT THIS PERIODT!!!!!

Written by

## Patricia Yvette Hunter

Illustrated by Silver Star

**I Don't Want this Periodt!!!!!**

© June 8, 2022

Patricia Hunter

Illustrations by: Silver Lining

ISBN# 978-1-953526-34-2



Published by TaylorMade Publishing
Jacksonville, FL
www.TaylorMadePublishingFL.com
(904) 323-1334

TaylorMade Publishing

I can't wear my white jeans or white pretty white dress.
Because what if it comes through? Everyone will know.

Not to mention, the products that I have to get from the store. It seems as though everyone is watching me pick out that blue and white box or that purple package.

There are too many to pick from! I just want to hide behind the shelves.

Which one will fit in my purse?
I hope no one sees it.
It's too bulky.
Everyone will know.

DiD i TELL YOU THAT
i HATE THIS,
PERIODT?

My head is throbbing and my tummy hurts so badly,
I can hardly concentrate.
I need to take something to help me to feel better

I do not want to
miss school tomorrow.
iT iS FUN FRiDAY.

Ok, I have to get my mind together.
IT IS NOT AS BAD AS I AM making it out to be.

PERIODT

MY MENSTRUAL PERIOD HELPS
KEEP MY BODY HEALTHY. REGULAR
PERIODS REVEAL THAT MY BODY IS
WORKING NORMALLY. JUST IN CASE

Who knows, I may want to
have children when
I'm older.

I will talk to my big sister,
or another woman in my life
about my PERIOD.

I do not want to Hate it,

I want to truly understand it

and find ways to embrace it. PERIODT.

Loving my period.
For life.

# About the Author

**Patricia Yvette Hunter**

*Mrs. Hunter realized as a young adult that she wanted to influence the lives of young people in the educational arena. Her passion and her deep desire to assist students, both academically and mentally, was obvious early in her career as an elementary educator.*

*Mrs. Hunter served as an elementary educator from 1996-2006. She honored her calling to educate the whole child by returning to college for her master's degree in counseling. She graduated from Florida Agricultural and Mechanical University with a bachelor's degree in elementary education and a master's degree in school counseling and obtained her mental health licensure from Webster University. She is highly regarded by her peers in the fields of education and counseling.*

*Along with working as an elementary educator, she has also worked as a school counselor and a military student support specialist. Additionally, she is a certified youth mental health first aid instructor and a licensed mental health counselor. She has been in private practice for 2 years and is currently a mental health counselor with Clay County Schools. Her expertise in the field of counseling has landed her multiple appearances in print magazines, on local news segments, and Clay County school district news.*

Mrs. Hunter works with children from a variety of academic levels and socio-economic statuses.  Although out of the day-to-day classroom, she continues to assist a small roster of students achieve academic success. In her ongoing support of parents and students who have experienced trauma, Mrs. Hunter helps students access mental health services and social-emotional assistance when needed.  She is actively involved in her church, serving as a youth leader. Her desire to educate and assist the whole child is reflected in all that she does.

Personally, Mrs. Hunter is married to the love of her life, Forrest Hunter. Mr. Hunter is the epitome of a supportive husband and applauds his wife's passion to make every child she encounters, whole. She has a son who is a graduate of Florida State University.  Mrs. Hunter enjoys spending her free time with her loving family and friends.